Dear
Welcome to the world of

# Geronimo Stilton

THE RODENT'S GAZETTE
EDITORIAL STAFF

**Geronimo Stilton**
A learned and brainy
mouse; editor of
*The Rodent's Gazette*

**Thea Stilton**
Geronimo's sister and
special correspondent at
*The Rodent's Gazette*

**Trap Stilton**
An awful joker;
Geronimo's cousin and
owner of the store
Cheap Junk for Less

**Benjamin Stilton**
A sweet and loving
nine-year-old mouse;
Geronimo's favorite
nephew

# Geronimo Stilton

## MYSTERIOUS EYE
## OF THE DRAGON

Scholastic Inc.

Copyright © 2018 by Edizioni Piemme S.p.A., Palazzo Mondadori, Via Mondadori 1, 20090 Segrate, Italy. International Rights © Atlantyca S.p.A. English translation © 2021 by Atlantyca S.p.A.

The publisher does not have any control over and does not assume any responsibility for author or third-party websites or their content.

GERONIMO STILTON names, characters, and related indicia are copyright, trademark, and exclusive license of Atlantyca S.p.A. All rights reserved. The moral right of the author has been asserted. Based on an original idea by Elisabetta Dami. geronimostilton.com

Published by Scholastic Inc., *Publishers since 1920*, 557 Broadway, New York, NY 10012. SCHOLASTIC and associated logos are trademarks and/or registered trademarks of Scholastic Inc.

*Stilton is the name of a famous English cheese. It is a registered trademark of the Stilton Cheese Makers' Association.*

No part of this publication may be reproduced, stored in a retrieval system, or transmitted in any form or by any means, electronic, mechanical, photocopying, recording, or otherwise, without written permission of the copyright holder. For information regarding permission, please contact: Atlantyca S.p.A., Via Leopardi 8, 20123 Milan, Italy; e-mail foreignrights@atlantyca.it, atlantyca.com.

ISBN 978-1-338-68720-0

Text by Geronimo Stilton
Original title *Il misterioso occhio del drago*
Cover by Iacopo Bruno, Andrea Da Rold, and Andrea Cavallini
Illustrations by Danilo Loizedda, Antonio Campo, Daria Cerchi, and Serena Gianoli

Translated by Andrea Schaffer
Special thanks to Anna Bloom
Interior design by Kay Petronio

10 9 8 7 6 5 4 3 2 1    21 22 23 24 25

Printed in the U.S.A.   40

First printing 2021

# CALM YOUR FUR!

I left my house in the morning with a spring in my step and a twitch in my tail. I had a feeling that it was going to be a **mousetastic** day. My name is Stilton, *Geronimo Stilton*, and I run the **Rodent's Gazette**, the most famouse newspaper on Mouse Island!

What a mousetastic day!

When I arrived at my office, I heard **YELLING** coming from the editorial lounge.

"I want to go look for the treasure!"

**"No, I want to go!"**

"You don't know anything about treasure hunts!"

"I know more than you'll ever know about **TREASURE HUNTS**!"

"For the love of cheese, everybody calm your fur!"

What on Mouse Island was going on?

Who was doing all the shouting?

What was this treasure hunt all about?!

I hurried to open the door and get inside. I didn't want to be a worryrat, but the argument sounded serious! When I stepped in, I saw my sister, THEA, and my cousin **TRAP** fighting over an envelope.

Ouch!

**Thea pulled my whiskers . . .**

Owwww!

**. . . and Trap flicked my ear!**

Stop it!

**I yelled for them to stop fighting!**

I got between them, but that only made things **WORSE**! Thea mistakenly pulled my whiskers, and Trap accidentally flicked my ear.

**"OOOOWWW WW WW W!"**

"Sorry, Geronimo!" Trap said. "But you have to move out of the way. This is between me and Thea!"

"That's right!" Thea said. She tightened her grip on the **envelope** and glared at Trap.

This was ridicumouse! I tried to reason with these **SILLY** Fontina faces.

"Thea, Trap, why are you **ARGUING**? It's not worth it, I'm sure! Come on, put the envelope down."

But the two continued to yell . . .

"I saw the envelope first!"

"No, I did! That treasure is mine!"

"Oh no it isn't!"

At that moment, the envelope that they were fighting over fell on the ground. I stepped forward again and SCOOPED it off the floor. Rusty cheese knives! This envelope was actually addressed to me!

# DEAR GERONIMO STILTON

I couldn't believe they had opened my mail without asking me **FIRST**! "What in the name of all that is **cheesy** do the two of you 𝓻𝓪𝓽𝓼 think you're doing? This envelope clearly has my name written on it!"

**Parrot stamp**

Geronimo Stilton
8 Mouseford Lane
New Mouse City,
Mouse Island 13131

**Chocolate stain**

**Fancy pawwriting**

Still **fuming**, I looked down at the envelope. There were a few interesting details that stood out. I put my snout so close to the envelope that my whiskers grazed the paper.

**1** On the envelope, there was a stamp with a parrot and a tropical flower . . . **INTERESTING!**

**2** There was a strange stain that smelled just like chocolate . . . **VERY INTERESTING!**

**3** The address was written in fancy pawwriting that reminded me of someone . . . **VERY, VERY INTERESTING!**

All these things together really got the **cheese** wheel in my brain turning. Then it hit me! "Sweltering Swiss cheese! The stamp shows that this letter comes from Brazil. And the stain here is definitely **Brazilian chocolate**. And I'd recognize this **pawwriting** anywhere — it belongs to my dear friend Isabela, who lives in Brazil!"

I turned the **envelope** over and saw that I was right. Isabela had written her name and address on the back side. **Thundering cat tails!** I hadn't heard from her in ages. I wondered why she was reaching out. I couldn't wait to see what she could have written that had made Trap and Thea argue so fiercely!

Quickly, I pulled Isabela's letter out and SKiMMeD through it. **GREAT GOBS OF CHEESE!**

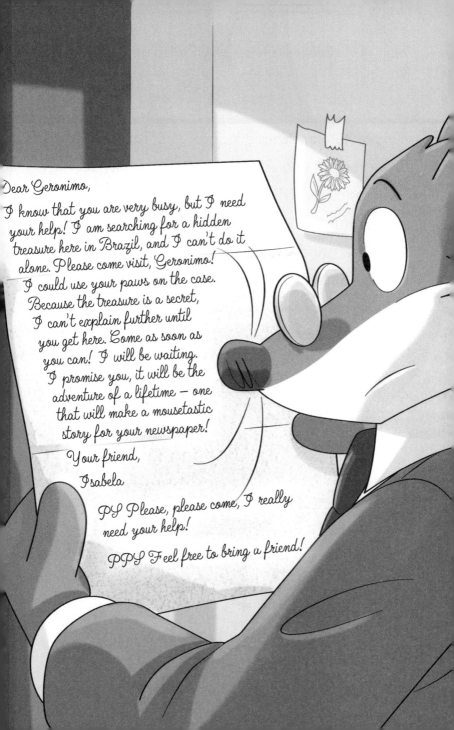

Isabela had written about an incredimouse hidden **treasure**. She needed my help to find it!

Hmm, poor Isabela really did sound desperate. I wanted to **help** her but wasn't sure I could get away from the newspaper. I had been to **BRAZIL** before, and it would be **mousetastic** to go back again.

I had liked meeting new friends, tasting new foods, and visiting beautiful **natural wonders**.

But I'd have to take a long plane ride to get there . . . and I get **TERRIBLY** airsick!

I do love Brazil!

SQUEAK!!!

# BRAZIL

Brazil is a country known for its amazing natural wonders, like the Amazon rain forest, which is famous for the diversity of plant and animal life that live there. The Amazon River also runs through Brazil. It is the largest river in the world! In addition to all the amazing nature found there, Brazil has many dynamic cities like Rio de Janeiro and Brasília, the capital.

**HOW TO GET THERE:** Brazil is located in South America, easily accessible from Mouse Island by plane!

**CAPITAL:** Brasília

**SIZE:** At 3.2 million square miles, Brazil is the largest country in South America.

**POPULATION:** Brazil has more than 200 million inhabitants!

**OFFICIAL LANGUAGE:** Portuguese

**TRADITIONS:** The Carnival in Rio de Janeiro is a famouse celebration that takes place every year in advance of Lent, a period of fasting that takes place before the Easter holiday. It is considered the biggest such celebration in the world, attracting over two million visitors a day. There are parade floats, dancing, and lots of music in the streets.

# FIGHTING LIKE CATS AND MICE

Just as I was deciding whether or not to go, the door of the *Rodent's Gazette* flew open. My grandfather, **William Shortpaws**, entered. He had a **furious** frown on his snout.

He **stomped** between us, waving his paws in the air. "I could hear all three of you **SHOUTING** from down the street! What

I heard fighting from down the street!

I won't have you ruining the good name of this paper!

in the name of the *Rodent's Gazette* is going on in here? I won't stand for FIGHTING among family members! Do you **understand**?"

He glared at each of us in turn. Nervously, I twirled my tail in my paws.

"Well, don't just stand there like **LUMPS** of cream cheese. Someone tell me what this fight is about!"

Thea, Trap, and I all started TALKING at the same time.

"Grandfather, this letter just arrived! There's a hidden treasure —"

"Trap pulled it right out of my paws —"

"Thea started it!"

"My name is right there on the envelope!"

Grandfather's **STERN** look faded, and he began to CHUCKLE. "Quiet down! I see why all of you are so worked up. A hidden treasure is a very EXCITING thing, indeed."

Maybe he wasn't so mad at us after all. I couldn't wait for him to tell Trap and Thea how wrong they'd been to open my **mail**.

"Well, Trap, Thea, and Geronimo, there's only one thing to do here . . ." He paused, and I **perked** up my ears. "All three of you should go together to help search for this hidden **treasure**. Then maybe you'll learn to get along!"

My **snout** dropped open. Next to me, Trap and Thea both groaned.

We began to protest, but Grandfather just **waved** his paws at us. "Enough! Thea: **YOU** will take **photos** of this trip for the *Rodent's Gazette*. Trap: **YOU** will learn new **recipes** that we will publish alongside Thea's photographs."

Grandfather turned to me. "Geronimo, you will write a **book** about this new

adventure that we will publish in installments in the *Rodent's Gazette* with Thea's photographs and Trap's recipes."

All three of us tried to protest. "That's a terrible idea!" we cried in unison. But it was no good. Grandfather seemed to be determined to make this a bonding activity for us.

Yuck!

Grandfather grabbed us by the ears. "Grandkids, you will do what I say."

"You will leave immediately, and that's that," he continued.

The three of us exchanged disappointed glances. There was nothing to be done about it. I guessed I'd have to 𝐅𝐎𝐑𝐆𝐈𝐕𝐄 them for opening my mail.

"Well, I guess since we're doing this together . . ." Thea started.

Trap continued her thought: "Maybe we should . . ."

Come on, let's make peace!

It'll be much better this way!

I finished the sentence: "Try to get **ALONG**!"

We hugged one another and then held out our **paws** to make a pact:

"We will WORK together to find this mysterious **treasure**!"

With that, we each went our separate ways to prepare for our **LONG** journey. We made a plan to meet up at the airport. Grandfather William had called in some **favors** to get us on the next available flight to **BRAZIL**.

Now that the adventure was about to begin, my whiskers trembled with excitement . . . Secret treasure, prepare to be found!

But my excitement quickly cooled into a sad cheese puddle on the plane. Thea could not sit still! She kept **jUMpinG** up to take "test pictures" of me and Trap.

"Say cheese, Geronimo! Look over here! Now look over there! But be casual! You look

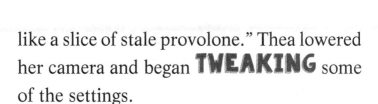

like a slice of stale provolone." Thea lowered her camera and began **TWEAKING** some of the settings.

Trap seemed oblivious to Thea. Instead, he seemed to feel the need to go through each and every cheese recipe he'd ever prepared in his whole life.

Thundering cat tails! All I wanted to do was draft the introduction to my book about this journey, and then take a **NAP**! But it

was beginning to look like that wasn't going to happen . . .

Finally, the two of them drifted off to sleep. Now I could rest up for our big adventure. But just as I was shutting my eyes, I caught sight of a strange rodent in one of the rows in front of us.

He had carrot-colored fur and wore dark glasses. He had on a crumpled raincoat and a wide-brimmed hat. I could tell he was watching us from the tilt of his snout.

## WHY?
## WHO COULD HE BE?
## HAD HE HEARD US TALKING ABOUT THE TREASURE?

# LET'S GO!

We landed at the **BRASÍLIA** airport in the capital of Brazil early in the morning. We made our way through the terminal and out to meet **ISABELA**.

Isabela is one of my very favorite **RODENTS**. She is smart and kind and has a fabumouse sense of humor.

She is one of my best friends, and I was excited to spend time together!

How nice and warm it is here!

My dear Isabela!

While Thea and Trap went to go get our baggage, Isabela ran to meet me and give me a giant hug.

*"Geronimo, how mouserific to see you again!"*

On Isabela's shoulder perched her pet parrot, **Bravo**. I reached out to pet him. "Bravo, you're as handsome as ever!" I cried. But Bravo only squawked and pecked my ear!

I couldn't take it any longer. I had to know more about why Isabela needed my help. "Tell me about this mysterious treasure!"

Isabela

HER PASSION
Cooking Brazilian cuisine!
HER SECRET
She loves fashion!
HER HOBBY
Exploring the incredimouse Brazilian forests.
HER BEST FRIEND
Her parrot, Bravo.
HER BIGGEST STRENGTH
Her fabumouse sense of humor.
HER FAVORITE DISH
Pão de queijo (Brazilian cheese bread).
HER FAVORITE PHRASE
Vamos! (Let's go!)

23

The smile dropped from Isabela's snout. She looked around, as if she thought someone might be *spying* on us.

"I can tell you a little, but we must be quiet in such a crowded place," she said. She leaned forward to whisper in my ear.

"Pssss pssssssss psssssss . . ." she squeaked.

"Huh? What are you saying!"

She WHiSPeReD again, "Pssss pssss psssssssssssss!!!"

"Excuse me, I still can't hear —"

"Are your ears filled with cheese?" Isabela interrupted. "I said that there is a treasure of enormouse value at stake!"

Psss Psssss Pssss

Suddenly, all the rodents around us turned to stare. RANCiD RAT TAiLS!

"Shhh, Isabela—everymouse

There is a treasure!

is looking at us now!" My fur turned **PINK** with embarrassment.

Isabela laughed. "You silly string cheese! I tried to talk softly, but you couldn't hear me!" She playfully swatted me with her paw. "You'll just have to wait until we get back to my farm to hear the whole incredimouse story."

Just then Thea and Trap arrived. "Oh, I can't wait to hear!" Thea cried.

"Let's get our tails on the road!" Trap CHEERED.

Isabela pointed to a nearby **red** jeep. "Everymouse inside and buckle up! Once we get home, I'll explain everything. *Vamos!*"

Thea and Trap HOPPED in the backseat

while I joined Isabela in the front. I had just settled in for a **QUIET** ride to the farm when she **PEELED** out of her parking spot at top speed.

I gripped my stomach with both paws. Oh no! I hoped I wouldn't get carsick! I hate going fast!

But Isabela didn't seem to notice my **distress**. She cranked up the volume on the car radio and began to sing along.

My fur turned a sickly shade of pale **GREEN**. There is no treasure that is worth this **WILD** ride!

**SQUEAK!!!**

I leaned my snout out the side of the jeep to gulp in some fresh air. Just then I noticed a big green jeep speed past us. It was going even faster than Isabela's jeep — if that was possible! The driver had fur as **orange** as carrot soup and wore dark sunglasses. I stroked my WHiSKeRS. He looked familiar. But I couldn't think from where! The only rodent in Brazil I knew was Isabela . . .

**WHO? WHO??**
**WHO COULD HE BE???**

# THE LAND OF
# EMERALDS

Finally, we arrived at Isabela's ranch. She yelled, "Hooray, we're here!"

Thea and Trap both cheered.

"The adventure begins!" Thea cried. "Isn't it exciting, Geronimo?"

I could only muster a small nod. My stomach was still SPINNING!

"Geronimo! Are you okay?" She looked concerned. "It's not my driving, is it? Some rodents say I go too fast." She LAUGHED, and Thea and Trap joined in.

"Oh, um, no. Of course not! I am just a little tired, that's all," I said. It wasn't a total lie — I really was exhausted!

I quickly hopped out of the jeep. "I'd love

a tour of this fabumouse ranch!" I said.

Thea and Trap climbed out of the jeep as well.

"I'd love to see your garden," Trap said.

"And I heard you keep cows!" Thea added.

Isabela beamed with pride. Her family had lived in the ancient house before us for generations.

"I'd LOVE to show you around!" she squeaked. "We do have cows and a garden, where we grow bananas, chocolate, coconut, and coffee. We also have chickens who provide us with plenty of fresh eggs."

But just as Isabela turned to lead us around, the sky overhead darkened. Lightning flashed and a heavy rain began to come down. Sudden storms like this are common in Brazil during the rainy season, but none of us were prepared!

"Every mouse inside!" Isabela called, guiding us toward the front door. As we ran, a bolt of lightning struck nearby, and all the lights in the house went out.

Inside Isabela's house, we stopped to catch our breath. Looking out a front window, I could have sworn I spotted a **strange mouse** watching us. He had ORANGE fur and dark glasses, just like the rodent I'd spotted on the road earlier. But I shook my snout to clear rainwater from my eyes, and no one was there.

"I'll light a candle!" Isabel said. "The

Him again?!

tour will have to wait. But I have something important to show you in my **ATTIC**."

We left our wet luggage in the hall and followed her up several flights of stairs to the very top of her house.

She led us to the darkest, dustiest corner of the attic. I did not like it up here!

"Last week I came up to organize in here." Isabela spoke in hushed tones. "As I dusted, I noticed this leather trunk, on which there

Follow me!

were the initials A.C. I realized that it must have belonged to my great-grandfather Abe Cheeseworth."

Isabela continued, "Great-Grandfather Abe was the greatest expert on precious stones in all of BRAZIL. His passion was EMERALDS. He even opened a mine in the center of Brazil that he called 'The Land of Emeralds.' Here he found a gigantic emerald, the legendary

EYE OF THE DRAGON!

But when Abe died, no mouse could find the emerald, even though they searched everywhere! It seemed to have DISAPPEARED forever. But . . ."

Shivers ran from the tip of my tail to the ends of my whiskers. "But . . . ?" I repeated.

Isabela grinned. "Let me show you!" She leaned down to open the trunk.

# A SECRET REVEALED

Isabela rummaged for a long time in the trunk. She pulled out a **MINER'S HELMET**, a pickaxe, an old **KEY**, and a *diary*!

Carefully, Isabela flipped through the pages and held the journal out to us. Someone had placed a photo of Abe Cheeseworth within the pages of the book. He had **THICK** whiskers and a broad smile. Under his photo was thin, faded writing. I leaned my snout down toward the page to get a closer look.

I started to read: "'*Do you wish to discover my secret and find out where the Eye of the Dragon is? Then you must follow your heart*

**MINER'S HELMET**

**PICKAXE**

**OLD KEY**

and be KIND to your fellow mouse. Or you'll be left with empty paws!'"

Isabela sighed.

"I studied this *mysterious message* for a long time, but I still don't really understand what it means. That's why I called you, Geronimo. You've **solved** so many cases, I thought for sure you could help me find this hidden **treasure**, too!"

I gulped. Isabela looked so **hopeful**. I couldn't disappoint her! But this message didn't make any sense to me, either!

I put my right paw over my **heart**. "Isabela, I will do anything to help you find

# The Eye of the Dragon

Brazil has many areas in which emeralds can be mined. I, Abe Cheeseworth, opened a mine in central Brazil that I call "the Land of Emeralds." It is where I discovered a gigantic emerald known as "Eye of the Dragon." The Eye of the Dragon is a very special emerald. It's an intense green color and larger than a chicken egg, making it very rare.

 10 - Diamond

 9 - Corundum

 8 - Topaz

 7 - Quartz

 6 - Orthoclase Feldspar

## The Mohs' Scale

In 1812, a famouse German mineral scholar, Friedrich Mohs, invented a rule for evaluating the hardness of minerals. He used ten minerals for reference and numbered them from one to ten according to these criteria: Each one could scratch the one before it and be scratched by those that followed. For example, talc cannot scratch any mineral, but it can be scratched by all the others, and a diamond cannot be scratched by any other minerals, but it can scratch all the others.

 5 - Apatite

 4 - Fluorite

 3 - Calcite

 2 - Gypsum

 1 - Talc

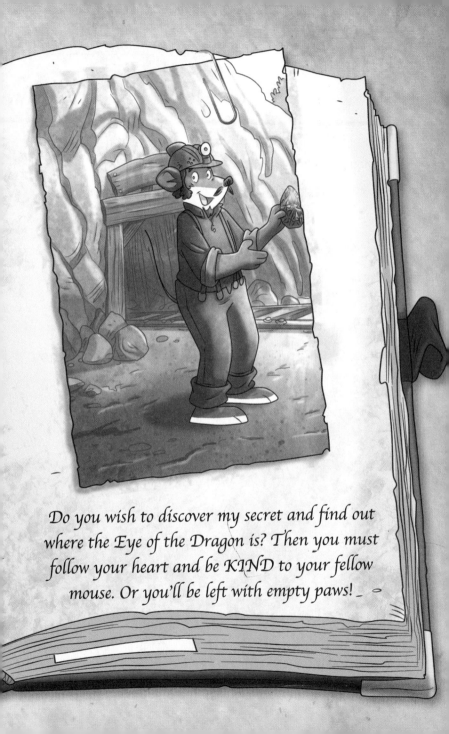

Do you wish to discover my secret and find out where the Eye of the Dragon is? Then you must follow your heart and be KIND to your fellow mouse. Or you'll be left with empty paws!

the Eye of the Dragon . . . *I swear on my family's secret mozzarella recipe!"*

Trap darted over and put his own paw over his heart. "And I solemnly swear to step in and find the **treasure** when Geronimo messes everything up." He grinned at me, but I scowled.

Thea playfully swatted Trap on the arm. "Well then, I also promise to help with the search, Isabela — especially because these

I swear on my family's secret mozzarella recipe!

Thanks!

two CHEDDARHEADS will probably mess it up!"

Isabela's eyes welled up. "Thanks, all of you. It means so much to me —"

Just then Isabela was interrupted by an enormouse crack of **THUNDER** and a flash of LIGHTNING. The windows rattled and we all jumped.

I was so surprised that I reached for Thea's hand and instead bumped into Isabela's candle. It fell right toward the fragile diary! Quickly, I dove forward and caught it just in time. Melty mozzarella sticks! It would have burned in seconds. And it would have been all my fault!

My whiskers trembled. *"Phew! That was close . . ."*

"Geronimo!" Thea cried. "You have to be more **careful**!"

"That diary is our only clue," Trap **grumbled**.

But Isabela waved her paws excitedly in the air. "Look! When the heat of the candle got near the diary, a *secret message* appeared. It must have been written in heat-activated ink!"

"**Thundering cat tails!**" Thea squeaked.

"I can't believe Geronimo's clumsy ways have finally helped us out!" Trap said, shaking his snout in disbelief.

"Hey!" I said. But I was SURPRISED, too. We leaned in to try to make out what had been written there.

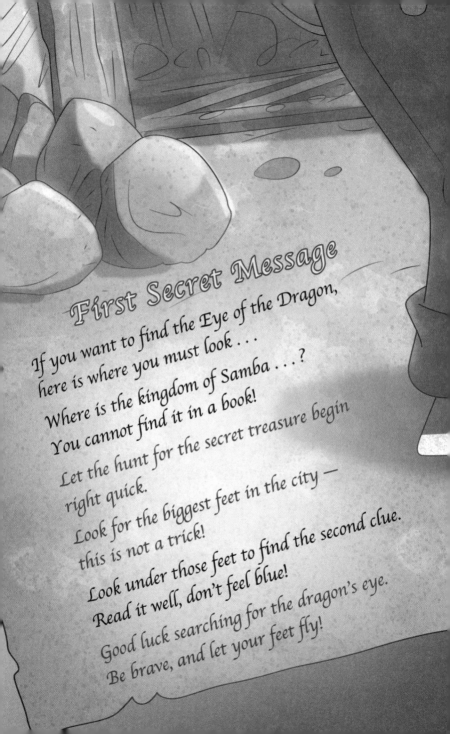

## First Secret Message

If you want to find the Eye of the Dragon,
here is where you must look . . .

Where is the kingdom of Samba . . . ?
You cannot find it in a book!

Let the hunt for the secret treasure begin
right quick.

Look for the biggest feet in the city —
this is not a trick!

Look under those feet to find the second clue.
Read it well, don't feel blue!

Good luck searching for the dragon's eye.
Be brave, and let your feet fly!

# But First —
# a Snack!

Thea, Trap, and I read and reread the riddle but couldn't make sense of it. A few minutes later, I heard strange noises. "GLBBB, GLLLGNNBBGG, GNLLGBGNNN . . ." "Sorry, guys," Trap said. "My stomach is growling like a LION. What do you say we break for snack time? Isabela, you wouldn't have any cheese-and-pickle sandwiches lying around, would you?" Trap looked at Isabela hopefully.

She laughed and tucked the diary away. "I have something even better — Brazilian cheese bread, or pão de queijo!"

Isabela led us back downstairs and into the ranch's large kitchen. A fire burned in the fireplace. Beautiful blue and white tiles decorated an enormouse indoor woodstove. After being upstairs in the dark attic, the kitchen felt very safe and cozy.

Isabela disappeared into a pantry room and returned with a basket of delicious-smelling cheese breads. *Yum yum yum!*

For a few minutes, the kitchen was silent, except for the sounds of our **H·A·P·P·Y** chewing. The bread was mouserific!

"These have to go into our article for the *Gazette*," I said.

"What a fabumouse idea!" Thea agreed. She got out her camera so she could take **PHOTOGRAPHS**.

Trap asked Isabela for the recipe, and she started to write it down for him.

"These are so good, Isabela!" Trap said, stuffing another piece of cheese bread

into his snout. "I can't wait to make them myself when we get home." He munched happily. "Hey, Geronimo, how many do you think you could eat in an hour?"

"I bet I could eat the whole bowl," I said.

"The whole thing?!" Trap insisted. "Let's see if that's true!"

I ate so many that pretty soon, I had the worst stomachache.

Luckily, Isabel brought me a *hot cup of cheddar tea*. As soon as I drank it, I felt much better.

10 MINUTES
Yum, how good!

20 MINUTES
So very good!

30 MINUTES
Fabumouse!

40 MINUTES
Maybe I should stop.

50 MINUTES
Oh, just one more.

60 MINUTES
And another.

AFTER 60 MINUTES
Too many!

## PÃO DE QUEIJO
### OR BRAZILIAN CHEESE BREAD

Pão de queijo is typical Brazilian cheese bread made with cheese and tapioca flour.

INGREDIENTS: 4 cups tapioca flour, ½ cup water, 1¼ cups milk, 6 tablespoons oil, salt, 2 large eggs, 1½ cups grated Parmesan cheese, 1 cup shredded mozzarella cheese

ALWAYS GET A GROWN-UP TO HELP!

PREPARATION: Measure tapioca flour into a bowl. Set aside. In a pot, mix the water, milk, oil, and a pinch of salt. Bring the mixture to a boil. As soon as it is boiling, turn off the burner and pour the entire contents of the pot onto the tapioca flour. Mix the liquid into the tapioca flour quickly until it forms a soft, sticky dough. Let it cool for a few minutes. Now add the eggs one at a time, mixing the dough well after each one. Then add the cheeses, and knead them into the dough until everything is well combined. Now it is time to form the individual cheese breads! To shape the balls, wet your hands with a little cold water. Use a spoon to scoop out dough and then roll it into golf ball–sized balls. Place balls of dough on a parchment-lined baking tray. Bake them in the oven at 400°F for 15–20 minutes.

I sat at the large kitchen **table**, sipping my tea and poring over the mysterious riddle. It didn't make any sense. There must be something I was missing.

Trap shook his snout. He was as confused as I was. "The kingdom of Samba? And the largest feet in the city? Great balls of mozzarella, I don't understand a thing!!!"

At the other end of the table, Thea was doing research on her computer. Suddenly, she squeaked so loudly that I nearly fell out of my seat.

"That's it! Listen up, cheddarheads. I've figured out the first part of the riddle. The kingdom of Samba is the city of Rio de Janeiro. Every year, at Carnival, they dance the samba for four nights in a row! That has to be it!" She slammed her laptop shut. "We have to go there, right now!"

Right now?! But I was just getting comfortable here!

"Vamos, Geronimo," Isabela urged me. "We don't even have to go back to the airport — I have a plane right here." She pointed a paw toward the window. Outside,

I could see there was a small plane parked on a tiny runway.

Gulp.

Thea and Trap grabbed their stuff and ran for the plane. I jogged along slowly behind Isabela. "Maybe there's a taxi I could take instead?" I squeaked.

Isabela just laughed and pulled me into the plane.

Just as I buckled my seat belt, Isabela took off like a rocket down the runway, and we lurched into the air.

"Rio de Janeiro, here we come!" she cheered.

"Hooray!" Thea and Trap yelled together.

"Heeeeeelp!" I squeaked.

I kept my eyes squeezed closed for the whole rest of the flight. When we finally touched down, I sighed with relief. Back on

Vamoooos!

Ugh!

solid ground outside the plane, I melted onto the tarmac like a puddle of cheddar soup.

"Geronimo, get up!" Isabela demanded. "I've brought you to one of the most marvemouse cities in the world, and you're missing it!"

I **groaned** but let her pull me to my feet.

"Let's go, Geronimo," she said. "We have a treasure to find!"

Are you okay?

Everything is fine.

# WELCOME TO RIO!

As soon as we arrived in the center of Rio de Janeiro, I began to feel much better. I could hear music so lively, it made me want to dance. I twitched my tail to the beat as we followed Isabela through crowds of people.

"Welcome to Carnival!" Isabela said.

We found ourselves immersed in a river of people who all danced to the rhythm of the music and they carried us through the streets of the city!

## CARNIVAL IN RIO DE JANEIRO

Carnival in Rio de Janeiro is a fabumouse celebration. There are many neighborhood festivals, lots of music and dancing in the streets, and mousetastic food. The main attraction of Carnival is the world-famouse Samba Parade in the Sambadrome, a special arena built as a parade ground. The very top samba groups from around Rio compete to see who is the best!

# - LA SAMBA -

Isabela taught us all how to dance the samba ... Now you can try, too!

**1)** Start with your feet together.

**2)** Bring your left foot behind you.

**3)** Then bring your right foot to match the left foot.

**4)** Now bring your right foot behind you.

**5)** Then bring your left foot to match the right foot.

The samba is a typical Brazilian dance that originated in Africa.

Who has the biggest feet?

We all tried to learn how to SAMBA. Thea and Trap caught on quickly. I . . . did not.

"Geronimo, what are you doing?" Thea asked, looking at my flailing paws.

"I'm dancing the samba, of course!" I snapped.

Trap shook his snout. "You look less like a samba dancer and more like a drowning rat!" He and Thea laughed.

"Let's stop joking around and get to work," Isabela said. "The riddle said

something about mice with **BIG** feet. Let's look around at all the feet we can find!"

There were many feet around us, wearing all different kinds of shoes. We saw shoes made of cloth or leather, with heels and without heels, with straps or without. Some were decorated with sparkles and pearls. Others were polka-dotted or covered in leopard print. We saw shoes of almost every color in the rainbow: gold, silver, white, black, red, blue, yellow, and green. Some mice had bigger feet than others, but none seemed big enough to fit the riddle.

As we looked, I caught a glimpse of carrot-colored fur through the crowd. Could it be that mysterious rodent I had spotted so many times? Was he following us? **Crusty cat tails!** Why would he do that?

# WHY?
# WHY, WHY?

Slowly, we made our way out of the throng of samba dancers. I was so tired, my whiskers DROOPED. What a day!

My legs hurt from all the dancing. My tail hurt from having been caught in a parade float. My feet hurt from being stepped on. I was a real piece of BURNT toast. And after all that, we were no closer to finding the treasure!

You ate so many pieces of cheese bread!

Oof!

You danced so much!

You got stepped on so many times!

Your poor tail got caught under a float!

My stomach gurgled because I had eaten so many pieces of cheese bread earlier in the day.

I had had enough!

"Why don't we take a break?" I suggested. "I saw a cute cheese smoothie place over there."

"Don't be a silly string cheese, Geronimo," Thea said. "We have to keep looking. Come on, I have a great idea!"

# THE MOST ENORMOUSE FEET IN RIO DE JANEIRO!

It turned out that Thea's great idea was just more walking around. We left the **parade** of Carnival floats behind and instead visited what seemed like every shoe store in the country.

"Surely they will know something about **BIG FEET** that could help us!"

But after many stops, it was clear we weren't getting anywhere.

Ummm...

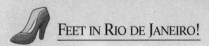

"How about the beach?" Trap suggested. "Most mice will have bare feet, which will make it easy to spot giant ones!"

No one had a better idea, so we headed to Rio's famouse COPACABANA BEACH. There were feet of all shapes and sizes there, but nothing that seemed too remarkable. We were getting nowhere fast!

"What if the big feet don't belong to a rodent?" Isabela wondered.

"What do you mean?" Thea asked.

"We need to think bigger," Isabela said. "Much bigger!" She wiggled her whiskers.

I shivered because her ideas are always **TOO** exciting for me, but she continued, "Let's fly, Geronimo!"

Before I could say no, Isabela had already headed off to rent a hang glider. I jogged after her. How bad could it be?

SQUEAK!

In minutes, we were strapped into a hang glider and launched into the air like a cheese pizza.

"Melty mozzarella sticks, we're so high up!" I yelled.

I'm afraid of heights! "**HeeeeeeLP!**" I cried, but there was no one around to hear me. Just seagulls drifting on warm air currents. They made flying look so **EASY**!

"Doesn't the city look fabumouse from up here?" Isabela yelled. "Geronimo, don't close your eyes — you'll miss everything!"

Carefully I opened one eye and then the other. My stomach did flip-flops.

I tried to concentrate on finding the secret treasure as we glided over the city. We could see everything from up here! We

passed beaches packed with tourists, parks filled with rodents out enjoying the weather, and lots of colorful buildings. But nothing that seemed like it was related to the riddle.

That is, until we flew over an enormouse statue. My jaw dropped. My fur stood on end. "Isabela! Look!"

She turned to see where I was pointing a paw and gasped. The giant statue had what we had been searching for: enormouse feet!

Isabela landed the glider expertly near the base of the statue, and we texted Trap and Thea to come meet us.

As we waited for them, I walked around to the front of the statue. How would we ever get up to where the base ended and the actual statue started? I twisted my tail in my paws. Maybe if I jUMpeD really high, I could grab on somewhere.

I bent my knees and gathered up all the **STRENGTH** I had. As I jumped into the air, Isabela came up behind me.

"Geronimo, what in the name of creamy **cheese** curds are you doing?" she asked.

Distracted by her question, I came **crashing** down! I rolled over a few times, and my paw knocked into a small, round indentation at the very bottom of the statue's base.

"Oof," I muttered.

"Geronimo, you did it!" Isabela said, pointing.

I turned my snout to see a **HiDDen** compartment that had opened and an antique-looking scroll that had rolled out!

This was another clue on this strange **treasure hunt**!

# Second Secret Message

If you want to find the
Dragon's Eye, listen to me —

Go to the land where the parrots flee.

Hunt for the next clue near a village
where they can cook

The very best feijoada — a recipe not
found in any book!

Then seek out a lovely garden over there

And dig under seven stones lit by the
sun's glare.

Good luck searching for the Dragon's Eye.

Be brave, and let your feet fly!

# THE LAND OF PARROTS

When Thea and Trap found us, they were *excited* to read the second riddle.

"This one is easier than the first," Isabela said. "We need to go to Pantanal. It's a nature reserve where you can find the most incredimouse birds: more than six hundred and fifty different species!"

We took a taxi back to Isabela's plane and headed to Pantanal.

Crocodiles!

As soon as we landed, we made our way to the river and rented a flat-bottomed BOAT.

"There's only room for three of us in the boat," Isabela said. "One lucky rodent will get to ride on these water skis."

"Geronimo, you should do the skis," Trap suggested. "It will make for a mouserific article in the *Gazette*!"

Before I could object, the others had HOPPED into the boat. Sighing, I strapped on the skis and signaled that I was ready.

*ZOOM!!* Isabela hit the gas and I was practically flying through the water!

Vamoooos!

# THE PANTANAL
## THE WILD HEART OF BRAZIL

The name Pantanal comes from the Portuguese *pântano*, which means "swamp." But this is no ordinary swamp. The Pantanal region is actually the world's largest tropical wetland. It is found in the center of South America, mostly in the state of Mato Grosso do Sul in Brazil and also partly in Bolivia and Paraguay.

The Pantanal region is home to an incredible array of plants and animals: 236 mammal species, 463 bird species, 269 fish species, and 141 reptile and amphibian species.

Animals like iguanas, anteaters, anacondas, capybaras, peccaries, tapirs, jaguars, and rheas call the Pantanal home.

The Pantanal is around 54,000 to 62,000 square miles in size — roughly the size of the state of Georgia!

In 2000, the Pantanal was added to the UNESCO World Heritage Site List, for its "exceptional universal value." Other landmarks on this list include the Statue of Liberty and Yellowstone National Park.

"Look at those amazemouse crocodiles, Geronimo!" Isabela called back to me.

I turned to look, and my whiskers nearly fell out they shook so much! The crocodiles snapped their jaws at me. "AHHHH!" I screamed.

"This is so magical," I heard Thea exclaim as she took pictures from the front of the boat.

I was very ready for the magic to be over! And thankfully, it finally was. Isabela pulled the boat over to a small cottage. From here on, the water was too shallow for the big boat.

Gratefully, I undid my skis and scampered onto dry ground.

"Geronimo, pass me that rope there, and I'll tie up the boat," Isabela called.

I reached down and grabbed what I

thought was a rope.

This was one strange rope. It was warm and scaly and – A SNAKE!!!

"Help! Help! Help!" I yelled. I had accidentally picked up an enormouse anaconda!

The anaconda opened its mouth **wide** and flicked its tongue at me. I was paralyzed with **fear**.

Fortunately, Isabela wasn't! She leaped out of the boat and ran at the snake, scaring it away.

I flopped onto the ground. "Phew!"

"No time for a rest, Geronimo! We must keep going!" Isabela cried.

To my **SURPRISE**, our next stage of the journey was on the back of water buffalos! They were not my favorite form of transportation, but Thea did snap a fabumouse picture of me!

By evening, we had finally reached a stopping point at a *small* village inn. phew! I was starving! Lucky for me, we headed right to dinner. We got to try two traditional Brazilian dishes: *churrasco*, which is barbecued meat, and *feijoada*, which is a bean stew. It was fabumouse!

Trap talked to the woman who had prepared our meals, and jotted down notes for his *Gazette* article. Thea snapped a few pictures of all of us eating.

## FEIJOADA

The name comes from the Portuguese word *feijão*, which means "bean." It is a stew of pork, beans, and spices typical of Brazil. It is generally accompanied by white rice.

As I was licking the last of the bean stew from my *whiskers*, Isabela leaned in to whisper something to me. "My great-grandfather always said that this village had the best feijoada in all BRAZIL. I've brought us here because I'm positive we must be close to the next secret message!"

"Let's start our search bright and **early** tomorrow!" Thea suggested. "The secret message said something about a garden with seven stones. HOPEFULLY that won't be hard to find!"

I groaned. That sounded like it would be as hard as searching for a specific grain of Parmesan cheese at a spaghetti restaurant. But we had come all this way — we had to try!

The next day, we searched the village for

a group of SEVEN stones. To my surprise, it didn't take long!

"Look!" Trap called, pointing a paw at a circle of SEVEN white stones that were roughly in the shape of a heart. "That must be it!"

He tossed me a shovel and I started to dig. With a CLINK, I hit something hard — it was a small **METAL** box with the third message hidden inside!

# Third Secret Message

You're getting close, don't stop now!
Go back to the mine, take a bow.

Pull the chain and go for a ride.

Let the darkness be your guide.

At the end is a statue made of rock.

Grab your prize, don't be blocked.

Good luck searching for the Dragon's Eye.

Be brave, and let your feet fly!

# INTO THE MINE!

We were headed to where it all originally began — the mine where Abe Cheeseworth found the *emerald* in the first place.

"Come, I know where the mine is located," Isabela yelled. "It's a bit of a journey from here, but you three are the most adventuremouse rodents I know. For you, it will be a piece of cheesecake!"

Did she know me at all?? I was beginning to think not . . .

Before I could squeak out an objection, Isabela had flagged down a passing truck.

"The driver says he can take us all the way," Isabela said, waving a paw for us to *hop* on board. "Geronimo, you don't mind keeping the *chickens* company, do you?

The driver says they can get lonely."

With a sigh, I climbed aboard. The journey was so long that by the time we had arrived, the chickens had heard my life story three times over! But finally, we arrived in an area of Brazil called **Bahia**. It is known for its many mines that are RICH with EMERALDS.

The truck driver pulled over to let us off, and then he promised to come back for us before Nightfall. Eeep. I hoped he would come back!

FINALLY, we were going to see the

mine where Abe Cheeseworth had first discovered the Eye of the Dragon. And maybe we were about to find it again!

Isabela pulled out the key from the trunk in her attic. Then she inserted it into the **rusty** lock on the door to the mine. It slowly opened to reveal a **DARK** and **dusty** interior.

My whiskers shook. I couldn't believe we had to go in there!

"Follow me!" Isabela said. She switched on her eLectRic lantern and motioned for us to follow her inside.

"The clue said something about a mysterimouse rock statue," Thea said. "I bet once we find that, we'll find the EMERALD!"

But after looking around for what seemed like hours, we had to admit that finding the statue wasn't going to be as easy as we'd thought . . .

Which was disappointing because I really had to use the bathroom! "Um, Isabela," I finally squeaked out, "is there a bathroom anywhere in here?"

Isabela pointed a paw at a door a few feet away from us. "You're in luck, Geronimo, it's actually right there!"

I darted off, but behind me,

ATENÇÃO
PUXAR A
ÁGUA!*

*I'm not sure what it says.*

*I'm sure nothing bad will happen.*

Heeeeeeeeeeeeelp!

Isabela called out a warning: "Just be careful of the GHOST! Rumor has it that the spirit of an old miner lurks in these tunnels, and that he enjoys playing jokes on SCAREDY-MICE."

MY WHISKERS TREMBLED.

I opened the door to the bathroom as quiet as a mouse, but nothing jumped out at me. PHEW! There was even TOILET PAPER, though it had been munched on by insects!

Only when I raised my paw to flush the toilet did I notice a sign written in **PORTUGUESE** . . .

Hmm, I didn't know what it said. Probably just something like "Please remember to flush the toilet."

I reached up to flush the toilet, but as soon as I pulled the old-fashioned chain, a trapdoor opened under my feet!!!

"Heeeeelp! I'm faaaalling!" I yelled. *Faster* and *Faster* I plummeted down a dark tunnel. It was like a long winding twisty slide — but not **FUN** at all!

Above me, I heard Thea,

Trap, and then Isabela all cry out. I could tell they must have come after me and were also sliding through the darkness.

**WHEN WOULD IT END??**

I finally landed in an old mine cart, in a dimly lit tunnel. Thea, Trap, and Isabela soon fell into the cart after me.

Only Isabela looked happy. "I know this seems strange, but I have a feeling we're on the right track," she said. She pointed a

We're on the right track!

Gulp!

paw ahead into the tunnel. "Look, I think this lever is how we get it to move!" She and Trap pulled down on the lever together, and the mine cart **creakily** moved down the tracks.

It went *FASTER* and *FASTER*.

"Heeeeelp, I want to get ooooout!" I screamed.

Isabela tried to pull the lever back, but it **broke** off in her paws!

Caw! Caw!

**EMERALD MINES**

Emeralds have been highly sought after precious stones since antiquity. The first emerald mines were in operation as far back as 1500 BCE. (That's over 3,500 years ago!) Today Colombia is the world's largest producer of emeralds.

"Geronimo, stay *calm*!" Thea yelled. "You're not helping!"

Isabela's parrot grew upset at all the shouting and began to peck at my ear. "Caw! Caw! Caw!"

"This can't get any worse," I moaned.

The mine cart shot through a dark cavern full of BATS!

Then the mine cart went flying around a **SHARP** curve and directly into some enormouse spiderwebs! **Yuck!**

"Eeek!" I screamed. I even heard Thea gasp, and she's not usually SCARED of anything!

Worse than the enormouse

Heeelp!!

spiderwebs were the giant Spiders who lived there! They had many, many, many eyes that glowed like giant, terrible Frisbees.

The spiders tried to crawl after us, but we were too *fast*. We sped deeper into the cavern and the light went even DARKER. Then, with a sudden CRACK, one of the wheels snapped off and shot into the iNKY blackness.

The mine cart ground to a halt in a deserted-looking tunnel.

Eeep! Was this how our long journey was going to end?

# SEEING EYE TO EYE

Trap, Thca, Isabela, and I climbed out of the broken mine cart.

"Look!" Thea said.

"Are the **SPIDERS** back?!" I cried, looking around the **DARKNESS**.

"No," Trap chimed in. "It's a DRAGON!"

Luckily it wasn't a real dragon . . . As I looked down at the end of the tunnel, I saw what everyone was so excited about: a big rock in the shape of a DRAGON. And where the dragon's eye would be, a beautiful green stone sparkled like nothing I had ever seen before.

"Great gobs of glistening mozzarella," I whispered.

Isabela let out a shriek. "**HOOray!!!**

WE FOUND THE EYE OF THE DRAGON!"

She scrambled up the dragon and plucked the emerald from the rock.

"Wow, it's enormouse!" Trap said. "It's bigger than an egg!"

A **RUSTLING** noise interrupted us. To our surprise, a strange rodent emerged from the darkness behind us. He had carrot-colored fur and wore black sunglasses, a crumpled RAINCOAT, and a wide-brimmed hat.

It was the same

mysterious rodent who had followed us at the beginning of the adventure!

Isabel **screamed** in surprise and clutched the **emerald** to her chest.

Trap jumped forward to confront the intruder. "Who are you, and what do you want?" he demanded.

Thea snapped one photo after another. "I thought this **MYSTERY** couldn't get any juicier, but I was wrong. It has everything — travel, adventure, treasure, and a stranger *lurking* in the dark!"

Slimy Swiss cheese, I could do without the scary stranger lurking in the dark part! My whiskers *trembled* and my stomach flip-flopped. **Squeak!** Who knew that a ride on a runaway mine cart wouldn't be the most **TERRIFYING** part of this journey!

# GREEN WITH ENVY

The rodent finally spoke. "My name is Squeaky Ellington and that emerald belongs to me! Take your paws off it right now!"

Isabela squeezed the emerald in her paws. "Forget it! My grandfather left me secret messages to come and find this jewel."

The rascally rat just laughed. "You are very wrong. The emerald belonged to my great-grandfather Berger Von Karrot, not to your great-grandfather Abe!"

Isabela **HUFFED**. "We'll see about that," she said. She rummaged around in her pockets a bit until she found the **photo** of Great-Grandfather Abe that she had brought with her. "See, this proves it!"

"No, this proves it!" the rodent cried. He

pulled out a photo of his own.

We all gathered around to look at the two PHOTOGRAPHS. Both featured mice in vintage clothing. Both mice were standing in a mine. In fact . . .

"These two photos are actually two halves of the same photo!" I cried.

"Not only that," Thea said. "Look what they're holding!"

It was the Eye of the Dragon Emerald!

Squeaky explained: "Abe and Berger were colleagues and friends. Together they found the Eye of the Dragon in this mine. Berger passed the key to the mine down through generations of our family." He reached into his pocket and pulled out a key identical to Isabela's. Only his had the initials B. V. K. for "Berger Von Karrot."

I looked very closely at the photos.

There was very tiny, fine pawwriting at the bottom of Squeaky's photograph.

"'The Land of the Emeralds,'" I read out loud. "'Here on this memorable day of July 13, 1858, we two colleagues and friends found an enormouse emerald that we called "The Eye of the Dragon"!'"

Isabela's snout dropped open. "They found the emerald TOGETHER? I had no IDEA. That means you're right, Squeaky — this emerald belongs to the both of us!"

**I gasped.**

"But how will you share a single emerald?" Thea wondered.

"You can't cut it in half!" Trap cried. "That would ruin the FABUMOUSE gem!"

Squeaky smiled. "I would never want to RUIN the gem like that! Maybe we could trade it back and forth? Then both of us would get to enjoy its beauty! What do you think?"

"Well," Isabela said. "That seems fair."

"Okay, but Isabela gets the jewel first, understand?" Trap said.

Squeaky's snout fell. "Oh, um, I was really hoping that I could have it first," he said.

An awkward silence followed. **Slimy Swiss cheese!**

But then Thea's snout lit up in excitement. "We're actually working on a big project about this jewel. Geronimo is writing a series of articles about our search, Trap is working on recipes to celebrate the cuisine of Brazil, and I'm documenting everything with my camera. And now we will also be able to tell the long-lost story of your two **GRANDFATHERS**! What better end to that story than with the news that you will be sharing the jewel back and forth? Isabela

Ummm . . . I have to think about it!

We could take turns!

first, of course, and then you!"

Squeaky laughed. "Okay, okay! You're absolutely right. Isabela can have the emerald first. I hope that we, too, become great friends!"

Isabela grinned. "I hope so!" Thea happily cheered. "Good! Now let's take a photo all together!"

# LET'S ALL TAKE A PHOTO!

I am the only one missing from the photo because I had to use the bathroom again!

# WHAT A MOUSERIFIC ADVENTURE!

Once our adventure in **BRAZIL** was over, we headed back to New Mouse City. Isabela decided to come with us. She was going to do a series of talks about the **fabumouse** gem.

After we found the missing emerald, I actually couldn't wait to write about it!

When we landed in **NEW MOUSE CITY**,

What a mouserific adventure!

we hurried right to the *Rodent's Gazette*. Thea wanted to go through all her photos and choose the best ones for the paper. Trap wanted to start recipe testing. I had already written several different articles about our travels, and I wanted Grandfather to read them right away.

"Back so soon! Did you all do as I asked — or did you fight too much to find the missing **treasure**?" Grandfather cried the moment we entered the office.

I shook my snout. "We found the emerald! And we have plenty of content for the newspaper!" I assured him.

"Let's see it, then! I'm a **BUSY** rodent. I haven't got all the cheese in the world to waste!" Grandfather said.

"They're all on my USB drive. Let me just get it for you —"

"USB drive! I'm an old-fashioned mouse! I need printouts, Geronimo! Printouts!" Grandfather barked.

Just then the door swung open and my nephews Benjamin and Trappy ran into the room. They came right over and buried me in hugs. I was so happy to see them!

"Don't be a worryrat, Grandfather! We'll help Uncle G print out his articles for you to read. We'll be back in two shakes of a cat's tail!"

They ran off to the printer. In exactly four minutes and forty-eight seconds, they returned with my articles all printed out.

"Each article works as a chapter in a book," I explained. "That way, we can print a chapter a week in the *Gazette*, and then afterward, we can bind them all together and sell the book!"

Grandfather grunted. "Well, first let's see if the writing's any good . . ." He took the sheaf of papers and sat down to read.

My whiskers trembled. I twisted my tail in my paws. Glittering cat guts, what if he didn't like it??

## SQUEAK!!

Finally, after a long stretch of watching Grandfather flip through pages and look **thoughtful**, he got to the end. "Well, well, Geronimo. I must say, this is better than the **cheese soup** you usually write." He pushed his glasses up his snout.

I *blushed*, turning my fur slightly pink. This was high praise from Grandfather!

"In fact, I would say, it's fabumouse."

"What what what??? Fabumouse???" I yelled. I couldn't believe it.

But Grandfather raised a paw in the air . . .

"Don't go getting a big head, Grandson. It still needs an ending. After reading this, I'm expecting **excellence**. Don't disappoint me!"

"I won't, I promise!" I said. I went right to my computer and wrote all day.

Just as I was finishing up for the evening, Trap and Thea came over for dinner. Trap wanted to try out some of his new Brazilian

## RECIPE FOR DULCE DE LECHE

**ALWAYS ASK A GROWN-UP FOR HELP!**

### INGREDIENTS:

4 cups whole milk, 1¼ cups sugar,
¼ teaspoon baking soda,
1 teaspoon vanilla

### PREPARATION:

Stir the milk, sugar, and baking soda together in a 3- or 4-quart saucepan. Bring the contents of the saucepan to a boil. Then reduce the heat to a simmer and stir the liquid occasionally, until it caramelizes (turns brown) and thickens. This will take a while — around an hour and a half! Be careful not to let the mixture burn. Once the contents of the pot look like a thick caramel sauce, turn off the heat. Stir in the vanilla and then transfer the dulce de leche to a bowl to cool. Serve as a sauce for ice cream, or use it as a dip!

recipes, and Thea wanted to show us a slideshow of her photographs.

For dessert, Isabela showed us all how to make a Brazilian dessert called *dulce de leche*. It's a yummy caramel sauce you can dip things into or eat over ice cream. We had ours with choco-cheddar ice cream!

After **dinner**, Thea gathered us all together.

"We need one last

picture to remember this fabumouse adventure by," she said. She set the self-timer and jumped into the frame with us as the timer counted down.

"Everybody say 'Eye of the Dragon'!" Thea said.

"EYE OF THE DRAGON!!"

# Don't miss a single fabumouse adventure!

☐ #1 Lost Treasure of the Emerald Eye

☐ #2 The Curse of the Cheese Pyramid

☐ #3 Cat and Mouse in a Haunted House

☐ #4 I'm Too Fond of My Fur!

☐ #5 Four Mice Deep in the Jungle

☐ #6 Paws Off, Cheddarface!

☐ #7 Red Pizzas for a Blue Count

☐ #8 Attack of the Bandit Cats

☐ #9 A Fabumouse Vacation for Geronimo

☐ #10 All Because of a Cup of Coffee

☐ #11 It's Halloween, You 'Fraidy Mouse!

☐ #12 Merry Christmas, Geronimo!

☐ #13 The Phantom of the Subway

☐ #14 The Temple of the Ruby of Fire

☐ #15 The Mona Mousa Code

☐ #16 A Cheese-Colored Camper

☐ #17 Watch Your Whiskers, Stilton!

☐ #18 Shipwreck on the Pirate Islands

☐ #19 My Name Is Stilton, Geronimo Stilton

☐ #20 Surf's Up, Geronimo!

☐ #21 The Wild, Wild West

☐ #22 The Secret of Cacklefur Castle

☐ A Christmas Tale

☐ #23 Valentine's Day Disaster

☐ #24 Field Trip to Niagara Falls

☐ #25 The Search for Sunken Treasure

☐ #26 The Mummy with No Name

☐ #27 The Christmas Toy Factory

☐ #28 Wedding Crasher

☐ #29 Down and Out Down Under

#30 The Mouse Island Marathon

#31 The Mysterious Cheese Thief

Christmas Catastrophe

#32 Valley of the Giant Skeletons

#33 Geronimo and the Gold Medal Mystery

#34 Geronimo Stilton, Secret Agent

#35 A Very Merry Christmas

#36 Geronimo's Valentine

#37 The Race Across America

#38 A Fabumouse School Adventure

#39 Singing Sensation

#40 The Karate Mouse

#41 Mighty Mount Kilimanjaro

#42 The Peculiar Pumpkin Thief

#43 I'm Not a Supermouse!

#44 The Giant Diamond Robbery

#45 Save the White Whale!

#46 The Haunted Castle

#47 Run for the Hills, Geronimo!

#48 The Mystery in Venice

#49 The Way of the Samurai

#50 This Hotel Is Haunted!

#51 The Enormouse Pearl Heist

#52 Mouse in Space!

#53 Rumble in the Jungle

#54 Get into Gear, Stilton!

#55 The Golden Statue Plot

#56 Flight of the Red Bandit

#57 The Stinky Cheese Vacation

#58 The Super Chef Contest

#59 Welcome to Moldy Manor

#60 The Treasure of Easter Island

#61 Mouse House Hunter

#62 Mouse Overboard!

#63 The Cheese Experiment

#64 Magical Mission

#65 Bollywood Burglary

#66 Operation: Secret Recipe

#67 The Chocolate Chase

#68 Cyber-Thief Showdown

#69 Hug a Tree, Geronimo

#70 The Phantom Bandit

#71 Geronimo on Ice!

#72 The Hawaiian Heist

#73 The Missing Movie

#74 Happy Birthday, Geronimo!

#75 The Sticky Situation

#76 Superstore Surprise

#77 The Last Resort Oasis

#78 Mysterious Eye of the Dragon

## Up Next:

Don't miss any of my adventures in the Kingdom of Fantasy!

**THE KINGDOM OF FANTASY**

**THE QUEST FOR PARADISE:**
THE RETURN TO THE KINGDOM OF FANTASY

**THE AMAZING VOYAGE:**
THE THIRD ADVENTURE IN THE KINGDOM OF FANTASY

**THE DRAGON PROPHECY:**
THE FOURTH ADVENTURE IN THE KINGDOM OF FANTASY

**THE VOLCANO OF FIRE:**
THE FIFTH ADVENTURE IN THE KINGDOM OF FANTASY

**THE SEARCH FOR TREASURE:**
THE SIXTH ADVENTURE IN THE KINGDOM OF FANTASY

**THE ENCHANTED CHARMS:**
THE SEVENTH ADVENTURE IN THE KINGDOM OF FANTASY

**THE PHOENIX OF DESTINY:**
AN EPIC KINGDOM OF FANTASY ADVENTURE

**THE HOUR OF MAGIC:**
THE EIGHTH ADVENTURE IN THE KINGDOM OF FANTASY

**THE WIZARD'S WAND:**
THE NINTH ADVENTURE IN THE KINGDOM OF FANTASY

**THE SHIP OF SECRETS:**
THE TENTH ADVENTURE IN THE KINGDOM OF FANTASY

**THE DRAGON OF FORTUNE:**
AN EPIC KINGDOM OF FANTASY ADVENTURE

**THE GUARDIAN OF THE REALM:**
THE ELEVENTH ADVENTURE IN THE KINGDOM OF FANTASY

**THE ISLAND OF DRAGONS:**
THE TWELFTH ADVENTURE IN THE KINGDOM OF FANTASY

**THE BATTLE FOR THE CRYSTAL CASTLE:**
THE THIRTEENTH ADVENTURE IN THE KINGDOM OF FANTASY

**THE KEEPERS OF THE EMPIRE:**
THE FOURTEENTH ADVENTURE IN THE KINGDOM OF FANTASY

# Visit Geronimo in every universe!

## Spacemice

Geronimo Stiltonix and his crew are out of this world!

## Cavemice

Geronimo Stiltonoot, an ancient ancestor, is friends with the dinosaurs in the Stone Age!

## Micekings

Geronimo Stiltonord lives amongst the dragons in the ancient far north!

# You've never seen
# Geronimo Stilton like this before!

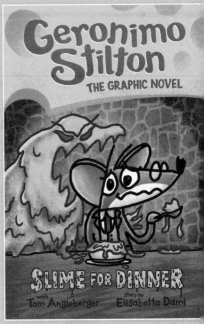

Get your paws on the all-new

# Geronimo Stilton

graphic novels. You've gouda* have them!

*Gouda is
a type
of cheese.

# Don't miss any of my fabumouse special editions!

THE JOURNEY
TO ATLANTIS

THE SECRET OF
THE FAIRIES

THE SECRET OF
THE SNOW

THE CLOUD
CASTLE

THE TREASURE
OF THE SEA

THE LAND OF
FLOWERS

THE SECRET OF
THE CRYSTAL
FAIRIES

THE DANCE OF
THE STAR FAIRIES

THE MAGIC OF
THE MIRROR

# Don't miss any of these exciting Thea Sisters adventures!

**Thea Stilton and the Dragon's Code**

**Thea Stilton and the Mountain of Fire**

**Thea Stilton and the Ghost of the Shipwreck**

**Thea Stilton and the Secret City**

**Thea Stilton and the Mystery in Paris**

**Thea Stilton and the Cherry Blossom Adventure**

**Thea Stilton and the Star Castaways**

**Thea Stilton: Big Trouble in the Big Apple**

**Thea Stilton and the Ice Treasure**

**Thea Stilton and the Secret of the Old Castle**

**Thea Stilton and the Blue Scarab Hunt**

**Thea Stilton and the Prince's Emerald**

**Thea Stilton and the Mystery on the Orient Express**

**Thea Stilton and the Dancing Shadows**

**Thea Stilton and the Legend of the Fire Flowers**

**Thea Stilton and the Spanish Dance Mission**

**Thea Stilton and the
Journey to the Lion's Den**

**Thea Stilton and the
Great Tulip Heist**

**Thea Stilton and the
Chocolate Sabotage**

**Thea Stilton and the
Missing Myth**

**Thea Stilton and the
Lost Letters**

**Thea Stilton and the
Tropical Treasure**

**Thea Stilton and the
Hollywood Hoax**

**Thea Stilton and the
Madagascar Madness**

**Thea Stilton and the
Frozen Fiasco**

**Thea Stilton and the
Venice Masquerade**

**Thea Stilton and the
Niagara Splash**

**Thea Stilton and the
Riddle of the Ruins**

**Thea Stilton and the
Phantom of the Orchestra**

**Thea Stilton and the
Black Forest Burglary**

**Thea Stilton and the
Race for the Gold**

**Thea Stilton and the
Rainforest Rescue**

**Thea Stilton and the
American Dream**

**Thea Stilton and the
Roman Holiday**

# Map of Mouse Island

1. Big Ice Lake
2. Frozen Fur Peak
3. Slipperyslopes Glacier
4. Coldcreeps Peak
5. Ratzikistan
6. Transratania
7. Mount Vamp
8. Roastedrat Volcano
9. Brimstone Lake
10. Poopedcat Pass
11. Stinko Peak
12. Dark Forest
13. Vain Vampires Valley
14. Goose Bumps Gorge
15. The Shadow Line Pass
16. Penny Pincher Castle
17. Nature Reserve Park
18. Las Ratayas Marinas
19. Fossil Forest
20. Lake Lake
21. Lake Lakelake
22. Lake Lakelakelake
23. Cheddar Crag
24. Cannycat Castle
25. Valley of the Giant Sequoia
26. Cheddar Springs
27. Sulfurous Swamp
28. Old Reliable Geyser
29. Vole Vale
30. Ravingrat Ravine
31. Gnat Marshes
32. Munster Highlands
33. Mousehara Desert
34. Oasis of the Sweaty Camel
35. Cabbagehead Hill
36. Rattytrap Jungle
37. Rio Mosquito

# Map of New Mouse City

1. Industrial Zone
2. Cheese Factories
3. Angorat International Airport
4. WRAT Radio and Television Station
5. Cheese Market
6. Fish Market
7. Town Hall
8. Snotnose Castle
9. The Seven Hills of Mouse Island
10. Mouse Central Station
11. Trade Center
12. Movie Theater
13. Gym
14. Catnegie Hall
15. Singing Stone Plaza
16. The Gouda Theater
17. Grand Hotel
18. Mouse General Hospital
19. Botanical Gardens
20. Cheap Junk for Less (Trap's store)
21. Aunt Sweetfur and Benjamin's House
22. Museum of Modern Art
23. University and Library
24. *The Daily Rat*
25. *The Rodent's Gazette*
26. Trap's House
27. Fashion District
28. The Mouse House Restaurant
29. Environmental Protection Center
30. Harbor Office
31. Mousidon Square Garden
32. Golf Course
33. Swimming Pool
34. Tennis Courts
35. Curlyfur Island Amusement Park
36. Geronimo's House
37. Historic District
38. Public Library
39. Shipyard
40. Thea's House
41. New Mouse Harbor
42. Luna Lighthouse
43. The Statue of Liberty
44. Hercule Poirat's Office
45. Petunia Pretty Paws's House
46. Grandfather William's House

Dear mouse friends,
Thanks for reading, and farewell
till the next book.
It'll be another whisker-licking-good
adventure, and that's a promise!

Geronimo Stilton